The day had finally come! It was the first day of school and I was ready to start the new year as one of the eldest students on campus. I had so many plans; but first on the agenda was to share my epic summer with everyone. I was 'fresh to death' in my new maroon foamposites, H&M distressed jeans, mid-sleeve black shirt and maroon puff vest. See, I take immense pride in my overall image. For as long as I can remember, I can hear my mom saying: "The way you present yourself in public shows people how to treat you." For that reason, fashion is big on my list of priorities. Sure, I'm only 13, but when your mom is

my mom...
appearance is key;
right up there with
morals and
education.

Walking onto
campus for the first
day of 8th grade was
as to be expected
and could be
described in one

word; pandemonium. Excited girls screaming to the top of the lungs when they saw their clique. The fellas were keeping it cool but eager to see their friends whom they hadn't interacted with in over 2 months. The usually mean teachers had real smiles on their faces, pleasantly speaking to students and parents alike. Clearly, this behavior was due to the long break they obviously needed after a long year.

The first bell rang. I entered into my homeroom class, keeping my new Jansport close. I settled into my seat and realized *SHE'S* finally in my homeroom this year!

I made up my mind in that moment that this year was the year I was going to do it. I kept it cool while I scanned the room as if I was making a spur of the moment decision. My eyes locked in on one of 10 empty seats and I acted as though I haphazardly chose the seat, which happened to be right next to her.

Wait! What happened over the summer? She and I look eye to eye now. Did I grow that much? Her caramel skin glowed like Beyoncé's; her hair was silky straight and flowed like a gentle summer breeze. She smelled like strawberry-shortcake roses and we actually had on the same shoes and backpack. I was sure I matched her swag today, and hoped to give her the same feels she gave me. I brushed my hair all summer long to have my waves dippin' like 360 Jezzy's. I even snuck some of my dad's Vince Camuto to make sure I smelled just as memorable.

I can tell from the start to my morning, this year is going to be better than I originally anticipated. I was ready for the first day of school routine where our homeroom teacher askes the class what we did over the summer as an icebreaker. I practiced my version of events several times to ensure I could condense it all into sixty seconds or less. After several mediocre stories, finally it was my turn:

"Hi Bobby, would you like to share what you had the pleasure of doing this summer?"

"Hi Mrs. Simon, Yes I'd love to share. My summer was

pretty awesome. I was invited to Orlando Florida to compete in the national AAU Junior Olympics track meet. My grand mom, uncle and cousins came down from Atlanta and my aunt and other cousins flew in from California with my family. Since it was during my birthday week; we celebrated my 13th birthday and they were all there to see me compete. The highlight of the trip was definitely Disney World and when my 4x1-relay team placed 6th overall. We each received these huge medals." As I said the last line, I pulled out the heavy, solid, bronzy medal from my backpack for a visual. The class gasped and oohed at the medal. Jada gave me a subtle smile that showed some of her pearly white teeth and I couldn't control the butterflies in the pit of my stomach. Mrs. Simon and the class congratulated me, told me how cool it was and thanked me for sharing. The nostalgic feeling I had almost immediately disappeared when I heard a snide comment from across my table.

"Black people travel and go on

vacations?" I could barely believe my ears, it was the most ignorant comment I'd ever heard and to make matters worse it came from Rex. I thought Rex and I were friends. Rex was a somewhat cool kid who I'd grown up with; yet as an eighth, grader had not perfected his times tables let alone string a paragraph together. I never judged him and I couldn't believe he would generalize me that way. Jada and Lucia both looked at me to see if I'd heard and I immediately identified with Jada's look. She was wondering what my reaction was going to be. My look to her was one that expressed I had no idea at that moment but I was going to do something. I had to weigh my options here because I liked Rex. Our parents were on the PTA and we've played together since kindergarten. As others shared their summer stories, I couldn't focus. I was perplexed. When did Rex take on this school of thought? Rex was white but I never thought we saw color in our friendship. Were his parents' racist? Could I really categorize this as innocent ignorance?

I realized in that moment I may be the most conscious thirteen-year-old there is to date, however in 'Trumps America' it's hard to give comments like this a pass for mere miseducation. Rex was smart enough to only allow Jada, Lucia and I to hear the completely crass comment. I couldn't make a scene in the moment, as I would be the one called out on the first day for misbehaving.

I'm smart enough to know now isn't

the time to address him; I'm also smart enough to know that he knows better. We attend school in Berkeley, California, which is one of the most liberal cities in America. He must know that comment is unacceptable.

I am being groomed for excellence in all aspects of my life and my reaction to this situation could very well derail my shot at student council president this year if I don't play my cards right. I decided to remain silent for the moment but decided I would address him for certain when I could. The second bell rang for us to dismiss and we all went to our respective next periods. I was uneasy about Rex's comment for the next 3 periods. When lunch time came I went to the restroom, got a drink of water from the fountain to collect myself and found Rex at the lunch table with his normal crew to address the issue man to man. Either others heard his comment and knew my reputation or Jada or Lucia discussed the disgraceful comment as it was clear everyone throughout the entire 7th & 8th grade classes were in the know. It was funny because everyone was not so inconspicuously surrounding us as I approached the table. Let's be clear, I didn't want to fight Rex. I am not the fighting type. I simply needed an understanding of what he meant by that? I wanted to confirm that someone I considered a friend didn't think I was less than he was just because I'm black.

"Hey Rex, have a minute."

"Hey sure, what's up Bobbie?" Rex stated in a very welcoming tone. His toned was as if he hadn't just made a comment that completely insulted my entire heritage during homeroom.

"I heard your comment about black people, not knowing they travel and all in class, and I want to understand what you mean when you say that." I said in the most diplomatic yet direct way possible.

He paused slightly, looked around and responded undoubtedly shocked that I had the audacity to ask. "Well... I.... I just didn't know you took family vacations like my family does. I'd never heard of a black family traveling during the summer. I always here about the financial stresses of blacks and I guess I meant I didn't know you could afford to do it. But... I mean...I totally think it's cool that your family does." As he looks over at 'his' peers for what appeared to be validation that his response was acceptable. To my surprise, they were all shaking their heads in agreement.

At this point, I was furious because he further insulted me. In the moment, I guess I could understand but to be stereotyped like this was very upsetting. In that very moment, I felt a range of emotions. Most importantly, I was grateful for my mom forcing my brother and me to watch every presidential address and speaking engagement televised of President Barack and First Lady Michelle Obama. In that moment, it seemed as though I heard the voice of my First Lady Michelle Obama saying: "When they go low, you go high." So, I did just that. I didn't let my feelings get the best of me. I paused, collected my thoughts and very matter of factly addressed Rex and all the eyes and ears that were locked into that moment.

"Rex, I think it's really sad that after all we've learned about slavery, Jim Crow and racism in

America you would think to make a comment like that. More so to make that kind of comment to me as your friend. All of the events, clubs and activities you are a part of, if you haven't noticed, I am also a part of. We attend the same private school, and I was on the same soccer and baseball team as you until I started running track two years ago. Being black is not an automatic dismissal from doing things that essentially all families do, which is love each other and make memories together. I've known you for over eight years and I want you to know I took offense to you making that statement.

Furthermore, I want you to be educated and know that anything you can do or want to do, I have the same right, access and privilege. My blackness doesn't preclude me from being a part of any of those experiences.

We are the next generation of leaders and you can't spread that kind of thought process to our peers or the next generation otherwise racism will never end."

After my 'presidential address'

I extended my hand for him to shake it to show there were no hard feelings. As I looked up the crowd that surrounded us included teachers, faculty, security and staff alike. All eyes and ears in the entire auditorium were lasered in on that moment. Rex extended his hand to me in an olive branch and the crowd erupted in applause.

"I apologize man... I didn't realize how rude and uneducated the comment was."

"It's cool, I accept your apology. Wanna play chess?"

"For sure."

Everyone dispersed from the crowd seemingly proud and clamoring about how I was so dope for the way I handled the situation. As we made it to the chess table and I slipped into my seat, I caught a glimpse of Jada's pretty brown eyes. She gazed at me like I've seen First Lady Michelle gaze at President Obama, and it was undoubtedly a very proud look of admiration. I matched her look and thought to myself this would be the most epic year of junior high ever!

28168382R00034

Made in the USA
San Bernardino, CA
06 March 2019